The Battle of Burdwan

NEEM BABA RETURNS

SRI JOYDIP

Book Name: **Neem Baba Returns**
ISBN Number: **978-81-966007-0-9**

All global publishing rights are held by

Sri Joydip Ashram
93 Itbhata Road, Burdwan -713103
http://www.srijoydipashram.org
editor.subhadip@gmail.con

Published on 5th June 2024 (World Environment Day)

Content Copyright © SriJoydip

DISCLAIMER

This is a work of fiction. Names, characters, businesses, places, events, locales, and incidents are either the products of the author's imagination or used in a fictitious manner. Any resemblance to actual persons, living or dead, or actual events is purely coincidental.

Contents

NEEM BABA RETURNS

6 NEEM BABA RETURNS

ACKNOWLEDGEMENT

Extreme environments are common these days. Uncommon are the leaders, who genuinely want to reverse the extremity of the environment. This Book deals with one such introvert contemplative leader, who has stood against the narrative of development, which is creating such extremity. This book is dedicated to such Neem Baba's, all across the world, who is selflessly contributing to raise awareness, on how we can reverse this extremity. The world needs more such climate warriors, than border-warriors to cope with the borderless world of extreme climate.

Preface: Who Breaks the Haradhanus?

Who can break this Hara-Dhanus which is considered one of the most difficult *dhanus* to take control?

What will be that bow, that can conquer this climate of Mother Earth and turn it as has been before? – Soothing, supportive, and temperate like "*Sita*" - the symbolic form of Mother Earth.

What will reverse extreme nature to its form of tenderness and politeness?

When will that polite rain wash away the germs in our minds, so that we gain the strength to overcome these extremes of nature, that are making life difficult for us?

I stopped at Durgapur for a while on the way to Asansol on Ramnavami day by car. With temperatures hovering around 40 degrees, the entire city center seemed to be on fire. Only the smoke of the fire, that red color is missing. This is not a burning, like catching a fire in a small place. As the body burns on one side, on the other side through the eyes you see the burning all around.

In the heat of some technology gimmicks and election campaigning, on Ramnavami, we have forgotten to seek real blessings from Ramachandra.

To be freed from the tyranny of this nature would have been a tilak of true blessing on Ramachandra's head, for the next five years.

Who will put that real Tilak on Ram's head? When can he do that?

Where in this election, there is a deafening silence on climate issues, as it is with every election.

No one is saying that we will break the bow like Ramachandra and defeat Vasundhara from Sita and free her from this tyranny. I only see people walking around with Ramchandra's placards. With the picture of Ramchandra, can't some of the lessons be taken from his life?

To satisfy his Guru Maharishi Vasistha, Ramachandra, at a very young age, went with Maharishi Vishwamitra to kill all the Asuras who violated the sacrifice of Sage Vishwamitra, to preserve the atmosphere of his yajna. On the way back, he won Mother Vasundhara in the form of Sita by breaking the Haradhanus, that too at the behest of sage Vishwamitra.

Who among us is that leader like Rama, who will stand up and slay this fiery demon, and save nature?

There are only placards, slogans, and guarantees. Where is the promise of 'net zero transmission'?

No one has guaranteed that we will clean the air, clean the water, and save the citizens of India from this fierce nature.

Everyone is promising livelihood, but as nature is getting more and more extreme, will we be in a normal state so that we can carry out our normal livelihood activities?

So why is no one talking about breaking the Shivadhanus of zero transmission and cleaning the air, which can save our livelihood, our health, and our Vasundhara (Mother Earth) for the next five years?

Tulsi Das's Rama of the 1600s, a strange blend of Sanskrit and Agadha, speaks of Rama's mercy. Talks about giving space to Rama in our hearts.

How can Rama's mercy of Dapar Yuga, work on Kali Yuga Prakriti's flaming remedy to break this 'net zero transmitter' and clean air by breaking Shiv Dhanus that can relieve many people from heat stress and heat stroke?

The real victory is for those who can calm that fiery nature.

Neembaba has come back from Rishikesh to Burdwan. The lone crusader is back with his baggage of purifying and healing thoughts.

Chapter 1: Ramanavami Night

17th April 2024, (Wednesday) G T Road, Burdwan

At night there was a noise breaking the usual silence spread over the Grand Trunk Road. It was the noise of the burning of a car, with heavy smoke around the sky. While in West Bengal, there was no usual tradition of burning big idols of Ravana on this Chaitra Ramnavami night. This burning symbolically seems to celebrate the victory of Rama (the righteousness) over the Ravana (the evil). A man was trying to escape the burning car he seemed to be choking for breadth. He was trying to breadth deeply but he was unable to do so. It looks like he was feeling breathless and after some time he fell into failing to get any support from anybody as nobody was around. A highway patrol car that was patrolling around the GT Road comes for support after some time and calls an ambulance. The ambulance arrives after some time and it carries the body into Burdwan Medical Hospital.

15   NEEM BABA RETURNS

Chapter 2: Murder Mystery

18th April 2024, (Thursday) SP Office, Court Compound, Burdwan

There was a thick tension in the room as the Superintendent of Police – Tirtha Roy walked into the conference room to meet with the press in SP bhavan at Court Compound, Burdwan. The air condition of the room was non-functional, due to some technical error, and over to the temperature in Burdwan touched a forty-five centigrade mark. So the journalist waiting for SP was sweating heavily and the small chit-chat stopped as SP took his seat.

Investigate Journalist Burdwan Times, Sambaran Roy had a strained relationship with Superintendent of Police – Tirtha Roy after he aired a controversial Interview of Dr Rahul Maitra on Neem Baba. He stands up and rubs the sweat on his forehead in the dysfunctional AC conference room of the SP office in Court Compound. "May I " then he sets out to ask his question asking his assistant Tillotama to move the microphone of Burdwan Times close to SP.

"Temperature is now 45C in Burdwan. Highest in last 70 years. And at the same time, the temperature is also growing in the Dr Rahul Maitra accident case. My first question to you – Is it an accident or a murder"

"Those are different kinds of temperatures. How do you relate with them ?" Tirtha Roy stops for a moment takes a break, and replies looking straight at Sambaran Roy. " Besides, If he drives in the daytime, then there could be heatstroke, with such temperature" Tirtha Roy gives a confident smile as if he has already sorted the case. "Though he drives an AC car so the chances of heatstroke are less. But he had a stroke as per the forensic report and his lungs were full of Sulphur oxide and Particle Matter below 2.5 microns which made it dysfunctional before. The stoke followed after this. So possibly he has been exposed to poisonous gas that led to a stroke. An investigation is still going on, and we cannot still confirm whether it is an accident or a murder "

" If it is a murder whom will you suspect? He used to have a very strained relationship with his wife Dr.Suhashini Maitra and recently got divorced. His boss Dr Gopal Subhramaniam is also very critical of him, he demoted Dr Maitra and made his wife the head of Sanjevaani Multispeciality Hospital. And he was dead against Neem Baba and he had attempted to make him arrested, wrote negative reports about him in the newspaper, and Neem Baba's disciples attacked his house last week? And he was going to meet Neem Baba in the middle of Ramnavami night when he met the accident. Are they working on a settlement plan and then he has been betrayed"

"Investigation is going on, we cannot comment on it right now. But this Neem Baba angle to this case, we do not think as relevant".

" But isn't all the motive of the murder there with Neem Baba? His disciples are annoyed with the repeated attempt of Dr Rahul Maitra to defame him. They have threatened him that if he doesn't stop on this he has to pay a heavy price on it. We have aired that video on our channel sir"

" Burdwan Times have shown a video where a crowd identifying as Neem Baba followers are heckling Dr Rahul Maitra. That is not substantial proof for murder charges. Besides we are still not sure that there has been a murder. You are unnecessarily fetching Neem Baba in this case. Anybody can claim to be a disciple of anybody and start running a social media campaign or heckle somebody. How is that person responsible for it ?"

" Is the police trying to protect Neem Baba in this case" another reporter from the back threw that question to the Superintendent of Police – Tirtha Roy.

Tirtha Roy becomes annoyed.

"But what is your problem with Neem Baba? Why are you putting Neem Baba in this case? Half of Burdwan goes to meet Neem Baba when they have problems. Why are you defaming him?"

"But does that make him immune from this Murder provided Dr Maitra has serious enmity towards Neem Baba"

"No comment further. You seem to have a propaganda, Mr. Sambaran Roy. We know Burdwan Times has been repeatedly telecasting programs against Neem Baba"

"No we have no propaganda. It's just that we want to have a healthy debate over the Neem Baba's ways of healing people. Is it wrong to have a debate in democracy?"

Tirtha Roy walked out from the press conference table without responding to anything.

Chapter 3: Investigation Journalism

18th April 2024, (Thursday) Burdwan Times Office, Court Compound, Burdwan

Samabaran Roy checked all the evidence again which he mentioned in his report about Dr Maitra's murder in the editorial. As he was looking at the laptop in his room, Tilotama his assistant joined him.

It seemed that he was missing something.

He looked at Tilotama and asked himself "First of all, why Dr Rahul Maitra decide to go to Neem Baba, in the middle of Ramnavami night? Dr Rahul Maitra never liked Neem Baba. He tried to arrest Neem Baba two years back when he was the head of Sanjeevani Multispeciality hospital. Now his ex-wife Dr Suhasini Maitra runs the hospital and was appointed as Head of the Burdwan unit of Sanjeevini Multispeciality Hospital by CMD Gopal Subhramaniam. What makes him go to a man whom he thinks as his arch-rival and fight against whom has made him lose his position and power".

"Yes, Why did Rahul Maitra have to go in the middle of the Ramanavami night to meet Neem Baba" Tilottama responded "That is a pivotal question for this case it seems like Ravana is burned in Ramnavami night".

"And who is this Ravana Tillotama ? - Dr Rahul Maitra"

" If the local people think that Neem Baba is there Rama, then Dr Rahul Maitra has to be the Ravana"

" Stop this nonsense of Rama and Ravana and focus on the case. One option can be he has come to know about something that he wanted to share with Neem Baba urgently" Sambaran Roy looked doubtfully at the whiteboard where he is trying to put together all the links of the case together in his chamber.

The office assistant knocked on the door. He asked "Tea or Coffee?"

"Tilotama would you like to have some tea"?.

"No Sir I want to leave early today. I came very early and spent a lot of time on the SP's press conference"

" Did you capture the photos of the accident venue and press conference. I want to use one of the photos in my editorial cover picture. It has to be a very high resolution".

" Sir, that will not be a problem, I will WhatsApp you after going through all the images in my house".

" That's the point" Sambaran Roy noded his head.

" What?" Tilottama was surprised.

"Just like you are sending photos in WhatsApp, many not-so-important work can be done remotely these days. So if it is not that important Dr Rahul Maitra can communicate through phone or WhatsApp. Why does he have to drive a car and travel three km, even knowing Neem Baba rarely meets with people at night".

"Why Neem Baba doesn't meet people at Night?"

"No particular reason and not like Dr Rahul Maitra, probably because he is a disciplined man and sleeps at night"

"Had Neem Baba attended the call of Dr Rahul Maitra ?"

"No, I checked the call was picked up by his attendant. The attendant said that Dr Rahul Maitra was tensed and nervous. He said he came to know a big secret about a very powerful man and his life is under threat and he wants to meet Neem Baba now, otherwise, he will not be able to meet him again."

"What did Neem Baba say?"

"The attendant was angry because he disturbing Neem Baba and he asked him to disconnect the phone. But Neem Baba overheard everything and asked him to come"

"But he never came. At 3 am Neem Baba asked the attendant to call Dr Rahul Maitra and asked him when he was coming."

His phone went on ringing and then the attendant called Dr Suhasini Maitra. She said Dr Maitra expired a few hours back with an accident. He was coming to see Neem Baba.

"Yes. Nobody knows why he is coming to see Neem Baba for whom he had so much hatred".

" Only Neem Baba can know that. Why don't we set an appointment with Neem Baba himself".

"You know Tilottama after we aired that interview where Dr Rahul Maitra made several charges against Neem Baba, he is upset with me. I don't think he will like to meet a journalist from Burdwan Times".

 "But Dr Rahul Maitra is no more now."

" I checked with his attendant. They have said Neem Baba has been upset because we have not checked with him and added his viewpoint over those allegations and just aired them."

" So how do we start our investigation."

" We try to find clues from the accident venue"

Chapter 4: Unfolding the Secret

19th April, 2024. (Friday) GT Road close to Elysian Campus

Sambaran Roy and Tillotama visited the accident venue, to find more clues on Dr Rahul Maitra's case. Tillotama kept on looking at Sambarana with some secret admiration, However, Sambaran's eye grew larger with surprise as he found that the accident venue was so close to the Elysian campus of Adani Corporation. They had recently erected a Pesticide factory on that campus. Burdwan being the 'rice bowl of Bengal' a Pesticide factory, would help to increase the production and storage, which were around Burdwan. Priya Adani the daughter of Industrial tycoon Satyananda Adani strategized Burdwan to be one of the strategic locations to grow there food allied Industry. One of the core businesses of Satyananada Adani was always working on optimizing the food chain, and that only has fetched him to the Forbes list of the most powerful 100 people in India. Sambaran had read all about this Elysian campus in the National daily but this was the first time he visited here. As Tillotama continued with her gaze to Sambaran she spotted that Sambaran was in a deep dilemma.

Dilemmas are common to Sambaran Roy. A journalist driven by a commitment to truth, grappled with a dilemma when airing Dr Rahul

Maitra's interview where he claimed Neem Baba is paying a heavy sum of money to his patient for giving false testimonials of healing with Neem Leaves. This money has been provided by his student – Dr. Gopal Subharmaniam from legitimate patient fees from Sanjeeveeni Hospital to convince people that Neem Baba is doing wonders with Neem leaves. He was demoted and thrown out from Sanjeevani Hospital as he protested this corrupt practice. The scam became popular as the "Cash for healing claims" scam and Dr Rahul Maitra expected that it would be a catastrophe for Neem Baba's public image. Neem Baba never came in public on this issue, nor did he say anything accepting or rejecting it. But Dr. Gopal Subharamaniam came on heavily on Dr Rahul Maitra, and his lawyers made a defamation case against both Sambaran and Dr Rahul Maitra. Neem baba remained as popular as he was earlier, and many people on social media came protesting that they had never received any money from Neem Baba for endorsing Neem Baba's healing capability and spreading the word of mouth".

Though Dr Rahul Maitra was a temperamental man and had many enemies due to his behavior he was a good friend of Sambaran Roy. The moment he saw the factory he could find the link between the factory and the poisonous gas which was found in Dr Maitra's lungs. Sambaran Roy had a deep question in his mind " Are those gases leaked from this factory".

He looked curiously at Tillotama and said " Are you thinking in the same line as I am thinking ?"

"Yes, there can be some relation between the poisonous gases found in Dr. Rahul Maitra's lungs and the pesticide factory on the Elysian campus".

" You know the meaning – Elysian?"

" Bliss"

"This is suffering for the whole city covered with such beautiful words".

" I think Satyananda Adani is expected to be here today," Tillotama remarked.

"They have sent a press release note in the email, but there is not going to be any press conference. They just stated the same thing which they put in their webpages a kind of fake news alert. Whatever is told against their company is all fake and fabricated news. Aree .. How do we know it's fake or real if it is not verified? Only journalists who have no intellectual self-respect will buy their thoughts"

The visit of Satyananda Adani and his daughters to the Elysian campus had ignited Sambaran's curiosity further, but the violent treatment and expulsion of reporters from the premises raised concerns in his mind.

One of the men from the private army shouted to the journalist very rudely as if he wanted to drive all of them out.

"We have sent the press release in your emails you can write a story derived from it. Mr. Satyananda Adani and his daughter will be not available for an Interview or press conference today. You can leave the campus now"

The journalist was upset. At the same time, Sambaran was torn between his passion for investigative journalism and the ethical implications of pursuing this particular story in a guerrilla mode. The red flags waving in his mind served as a warning, urging him to delve deeper and uncover the truth hidden within the walls of the Elysian campus.

His dilemma grew more intense with each passing moment. Should he risk his reputation and safety to expose potential wrongdoing? Could he afford to turn a blind eye to the threats faced by his fellow journalists? Sambaran knew that his decision would shape not only his career but also the lives of those who relied on him to shed light on the dark corners of society.

Deep in thought, Sambaran wrestled with his conscience, acutely aware that the path he chose would have far-reaching consequences. The weight of his choice mirrored the weight of the suspense and thrill that enveloped East Burdwan, both wrestling with the question of how far one should go in the pursuit of truth and justice.

Accompanied by his trusted photographer, Tillotama, Sambaran arrived at the Adani Corporation's Elysian campus, seeking an interview with Satyananda Adani and his daughters for the Burdwan Times. However, instead of a warm reception, they were met with hostility from a private army protecting the premises. Something was amiss, and Sambaran couldn't shake off the feeling that there were secrets hidden within the walls of the Adani Corporation.

Determined to uncover the truth, Sambaran contemplated the extent to which he should go in his pursuit of investigative journalism. Should he resort to covert means to expose the secrets of the powerful Adani Corporation? Was it ethical to disguise themselves as tea and biscuit sellers, concealing tiny cameras within their merchandise to discreetly capture the activities within the campus?

The weight of his decision pressed heavily upon Sambaran's conscience. On one hand, there was a responsibility to bring forth the truth, to hold the powerful accountable, and to shed light on any potential wrongdoings. On the other hand, there were journalistic ethics to consider. Covert means, albeit in the pursuit of truth, straying into a gray area.

As he looked into Tillotama's eyes, he saw her unwavering determination. She shared his passion for exposing the truth, and together, they uncovered many hidden stories that had made a significant impact. The thought of their shared purpose and the potential impact of their investigative journalism gave Sambaran a glimmer of reassurance.

In the end, Sambaran made his decision. He understood that the pursuit of truth sometimes required unconventional methods. The secrets of the Adani Corporation needed to be brought to light, not just for the sake of the public's right to know, but also to ensure transparency and accountability within the powerful realms of corporate influence.

With a mixture of apprehension and determination, Sambaran and Tillotama donned their disguises and ventured into the Elysian campus once more. The tiny cameras hidden within their merchandise were tools of truth, capturing evidence that would expose any wrongdoing and provide a voice to those affected.

As they embarked on this covert mission, Sambaran couldn't help but acknowledge the weight of their responsibility. Ethical dilemmas would continue to haunt him, but he believed that the power of journalism lay in its ability to uncover the truth, bring justice, and create a more transparent society.

And so, Sambaran Roy and Tillotama stepped into the shadows, driven by their unwavering commitment to investigative journalism and the pursuit of truth. The secrets of the Adani Corporation would soon be unveiled, and their actions would spark a necessary conversation about ethics, power, and the role of journalists in an ever-evolving world.

As they set up their makeshift stall near the entrance, the atmosphere around them felt tense. The private army, dressed in their intimidating black uniforms, patrolled the premises with unwavering vigilance. Sambaran and Tillotama had to be cautious, ensuring they blended in seamlessly with the other vendors.

As the day progressed, they observed the employees emerging from the heavily guarded gates. All of them wore the distinct gas masks, their eyes shielded behind the transparent visors. The sight sent shivers down Sambaran's spine, realizing the potential danger lurking within the walls of the campus.

Sambaran Roy: (whispering) Tillotama, did you see that? Everyone inside the Adani campus is wearing gas masks. This is getting more suspicious by the minute.

Tillotama Banerjee: (in a hushed tone) I noticed that too, Sambaran. It's highly unusual for a pesticide factory to have all its employees wearing gas masks. Something dangerous must be going on inside those walls.

Sambaran Roy: (adjusting his spy camera) Our instincts were right, Tillotama. The lack of local employees and the constant surveillance suggests that they are hiding something. And those spies dressed as ordinary people outside the campus, alerting the private army, only confirms it.

With nimble fingers, Tillotama discreetly captured photos of the gas masks, the segregated quarters, and any unusual activities she could spot. They knew that these pieces of evidence would be crucial in unraveling the mystery behind the Adani Corporation's operations.

Just as they were about to wrap up their surveillance for the day, a commotion erupted near the main entrance. Sambaran turned his attention, his heart pounding in his chest. He saw a group of local environment activists from East Burdwan Greenary Foundation, protesting against the corporation's activities. Their banners and chants demanded answers and justice.

In an instant, the private army swooped in, forcefully dispersing the protesters. The situation escalated quickly, and chaos ensued.

Tillotama Banerjee: (nervously) This is beyond anything we've ever encountered, Sambaran. We need to be careful, or we might end up compromising ourselves and our mission.

Sambaran Roy: (determined) I agree, Tillotama. We can't afford to be reckless. Our goal is to uncover the truth and shed light on what's happening within those walls, without endangering ourselves or the people of Burdwan.

Tillotama Banerjee: (whispering) Sambaran, we should capture as much evidence as possible. The gas masks, the segregated quarters, the lack of local employees—these are all pieces of a puzzle. The world needs to know what's happening here.

Sambaran Roy: (nodding) You're right, Tillotama. The puzzle is slowly coming together, but we need more solid evidence. We have to capture photos, record videos, and do anything that can expose the truth behind this enigma.

Sambaran and Tillotama realized that this was their chance. Amidst the distraction, they discreetly captured photos and videos of the clash, documenting the brutality of the private army.

Suddenly, an alarm blared, causing panic among the employees and the private army. Sambaran and Tillotama exchanged alarmed glances, unsure of what was happening. The campus descended into chaos as people scurried for cover, the air thick with confusion and fear.

Taking advantage of the chaos, Sambaran and Tillotama hurriedly packed their spy equipment and made their way towards the exit, blending in with the frantic crowd. They couldn't risk being discovered or detained by the private army.

Tillotama Banerjee: (looking around cautiously) Sambaran, do you think the gas masks indicate the presence of a poisonous gas? Is the entire town at risk?

Sambaran Roy: (thoughtfully) It's a possibility, Tillotama. The gas masks suggest that something hazardous is being produced or released within the campus. If that's the case, the safety of the town and its people could be in jeopardy. This is a Pesticide factory do you remember the Bhopal Gas Tragedy where a poisonous gas was stored from which pesticides were produced?

Tillotama Banerjee: (concerned)   Yes it's Methayle Isocyanate. That has been a highly combustible gas. It is stored in liquid but the gas chamber can burst at high temperatures. But we can't let that happen, here Sambaran. We must bring this information to the authorities, to the people who can take action and ensure the safety of Burdwan.

Sambaran Roy: (resolute) Absolutely,

Outside the campus, they found refuge in a nearby café, catching their breath and reviewing the footage they had captured. The scenes they witnessed were more alarming than they had imagined. The clash, the gas masks, the segregated quarters—it all pointed towards a grave secret hidden within the Adani Corporation's Elysian campus.

Sambaran Roy: Tillotama, Our duty as journalists is not just to report the news but also to protect the welfare of our community. We will gather all the evidence we can expose the truth, and let the world see what lies behind those walls.

Tillotama Banerjee: (whispering) Sambaran, we have to be cautious. We are playing a dangerous game, and we can't afford any mistakes. Our lives and the lives of those who rely on us are at stake.

Sambaran Roy: (taking a deep breath) I understand, Tillotama. We will tread carefully, step by step. We'll continue our disguise as the tea and biscuit sellers, capturing every detail we can. The suspense and thrill of this investigation are unlike anything we've experienced before, but we must stay focused and determined.

Tillotama Banerjee: (with determination) Together, Sambaran, we will uncover the truth. We will expose the secrets hidden within the Adani campus, no matter the risks involved. The people of Burdwan deserve to know what's happening in their backyard.

As Sambaran and Tillotama continued their undercover operation, the weight of the suspense and thrill bore down upon them. The adrenaline surged through their veins, fueling their determination to bring the truth to light. Little did they know the dangers that awaited them, but they were prepared to face whatever challenges came their way in the pursuit of justice and the safety of their community.

Their hearts raced with a mixture of fear and excitement, knowing that they were on the brink of exposing something monumental. They knew the risks involved, and the potential repercussions, but their determination to bring the truth to light burned brighter than ever.

As the sun set over East Burdwan, Sambaran and Tillotama knew that their investigation had only just begun. The suspense and thrill of their mission pushed them further, fueling their commitment to unravel the mysteries of the Elysian campus and protect the people from the potential dangers lurking within.

They were ready to face the consequences, ready to shine a light on the truth, and ready to bring justice to those who had been deceived and endangered. The journey ahead would be treacherous, but they were prepared to go to any lengths to expose the secrets of the Adani Corporation's Elysian campus.

NEEM BABA RETURNS

Chapter 5: A Looming Threat

20th April, 2024. (Saturday) Sinthala Mandir

"Our mental wounds are creating the extreme tone of nature's harp. Nature's harp is now playing in extreme tune". Neem Baba quietly looked at Soumen.

"The temperature is around 45 degrees all over Burdwan. At this time of Chaitra, in the courtyard of the sky, a silent temple could be found, where today there is a shower of fire. After the lively rhythm of the spring festival, the air in the sky is now the rhythm of the rain of fire." Soumen gave a poetic reply to Neem Baba's remark.

Young and restless is the dance of light, which even a few years ago in this scene of Chaitra, used to delight us. Now it is creating emotional scars.

In every grass, leaf, and tree, the sound of Chaitra's joy is mixed with the nature of this great heat wave. This is like a collective cry. The suns of nature have been summoned from the deep deserts of Rajasthan, in this lonely town of Bengal, to mourn the death of all the trees that we have mercilessly cut down over the years.

Their collective voices raise a tone of terror deep within our hearts. If this temperature continues to increase, then what will happen to us? Over the loud noise of the Lok Sabha polls, the unheard rhythm of a national disaster is heard.

Two other voices of Soumen and Neem Baba with this sonorous voice turn this armed rhythm into sound so that we can understand the future pulse of this current. Two men coming back from Rishikesh were discussing how an extreme Environment can create Mental Wounds.

After returning from Rishikesh, Neem Baba with his disciple Soumen stood at the heart of East Burdwan, his gaze scanning the surroundings with a mix of nostalgia and concern. The Burdwan he once knew had transformed, and the changes he witnessed weighed heavily on his heart. Divided into two districts now, the town seemed to have lost some of its essence in the process.

As Neem Baba traversed the road from Alisha to Birhata, he couldn't help but notice the lamentable state of the once-lush green cover that had adorned this path. It had been sacrificed in the name of progress, the trees felled to make way for broader roads. The sight left him disheartened, for he believed that progress need not come at the cost of nature's bountiful gifts.

Yes, the roads had become wider, accommodating the bustling traffic and the hurried pace of modern life. Yet, Neem Baba couldn't help but wonder if this was progress in its truest sense. Were these broader roads leading us toward a better future or simply widening the gap between nature and mankind?

His eyes caught sight of a towering skyscraper that now adorned the Burdwan skyline. It was an architectural marvel, a symbol of urban development and economic growth. New investors had arrived in East Burdwan, seeking to capitalize on its potential. They were bringing forth massive projects, promising a better tomorrow for the town and its inhabitants.

Neem Baba, once an esteemed Oncologist at Kottayam Medical College, had played his part in progress. He had contributed to the construction of a new hospital building, dedicating himself to the well-being of others. As a member of two development authorities, he had strived to shape a better future for his community.

But now, as a Sannyasi, he found himself in the depths of a serious dilemma. What truly defines progress? Was it the towering buildings and the influx of investors, or was it something more profound? Neem Baba knew that progress must encompass the growth of the soul, the nurturing of nature, and the preservation of our cultural heritage.

He yearned for a Burdwan where progress didn't mean sacrificing the green cover that brought solace to weary souls. He longed for a town where development meant creating a balance between man and nature, where the skyscrapers coexisted harmoniously with the trees. He dreamed of a future where investors didn't just bring financial gains, but also an understanding of the town's unique identity and a commitment to its sustainable growth.

Neem Baba, with his wisdom and introspection, was determined to find answers to his dilemma. He would embark on a journey to enlighten others about the true essence of progress, to ignite a dialogue that would shape a Burdwan where progress was not merely a façade but a deeply rooted and meaningful transformation.

And so, as Neem Baba stood amidst the changing landscape of East Burdwan, his resolve grew stronger. He would strive to redefine progress, not only for East Burdwan but for the world at large. Progress, to him, was not just about building concrete structures but also about fostering a profound connection between humanity, nature, and the spiritual realm.

As he entered the Sitala Mandir he found it still stood as a beacon of serenity amidst the bustling town of East Burdwan. His disciples have taken care of it so well in his absence for the last year. Its ancient walls whispered tales of healing and spirituality, drawing people seeking solace and relief from their ailments. Within its hallowed halls, Neem Baba, a revered healer, resumed his noble work, using the power of nature's blessings to restore health to those in need.

The air inside the Mandir carried a soothing fragrance of neem leaves, known for their medicinal properties. Soft chants and gentle melodies echoed through the chamber, creating an atmosphere of tranquility that embraced all who entered. Patients found solace in the presence of Neem Baba, their faith in his healing abilities unshakeable.

This unrelenting rhythm of environmental degradation has pained Neem Baba. He started his lonely mission, to do something that would reverse with the rain of grace the extreme climate of Burdwan. Researchers at Sanjeevani Multispeciality came to support Neem Baba on his lonely mission. Dr Abir Mukherjee with his colleague who has recently joined the hospital heard the story of Neem Baba. He was curious to meet Neem Baba and came to Sithala Mandir. Neem baba was sitting quietly and meditating below the large Neem Tree where the patients often gather to have Darshan of him

"Instead of patients today Doctors have gathered," Attendant Vishnu remarked. To many people around Neem Baba often irritates him. At the age of eighty-one, he remained continuously concerned about the health and wellbeing of Neem Baba. He always wonders how a man can eat so sparsely meditate half of the day and remain so vigilant to the concerns of so many patients around him.

Neem Baba overheard Vishnu's comment and silently opened his eyes.

"Vishnu Da can you bring chairs for them" he instructed him. Vishnu with a irritating face walked inside the Sithala temple as Vishnu went inside to bring a chair for both of them.

"We are ok this way sitting below this beautiful tree," Abir said humbly prostrating to him.

"I am not ok. I want doctors to be respected. You are in such a noble job of healing. People shall respect you. You deserve that."

Abir was speechless for some time over Neem Baba's silent and determined voice.

Vishu da brought two wooden chairs for Dr. Abir and Dr. Moumita.

Neem Baba quietly asked both of them " What brings you here?".

" We are researchers who have joined this hospital after our doctorate in environmental sciences. We are working on air pollution PM2.5 and PM10 and its effect on human lungs. Suddenly a few days back we had a Pulmonary Health Conference in Rajarhat Kolkata in Indian Pulmonary Health Institute. Dr Gopal Subhramaniam came to lecture at this conference from Chennai, and as you know he has been our top boss. We meet him during the lunch break and have a small chat, about where we want to focus. So he suggested I shall come a consult you whether with Neem Tree we can have any remedy of growing PM2.5 and PM10 pollution, which is affecting the lungs".

"We are getting many lung cases in ashram probably PM2.5 and PM10 is growing in Burdwan also in a big way. Of course, there is no analysis of the psychological damage that can occur as a result of these particles which are environmental stressors. Your research work and analysis is significant in many ways". Neem Baba replied in a very optimistic tone. This was probably one of the effective meetings after coming back to Burdwan and he was very concerned about the growing complexities of the environment of Burdwan in between and it's effect on public health.

Neem Baba: (with a calming voice) looked at Dr Abir and Dr Moumita." You have started a great work. Experience some of the real power of this unpolluted air of Sitala mandir before you go to learn more about the polluted air of Burdwan.

Breathe deeply, my child. Let the healing power of the Neem Leaf medicine flow through you. It will help alleviate your suffering and make you strong to handle this challenging project ".

In the morning session, Neem Baba stood amid his ashram, his gaze fixed on the worried faces of Suprna Roy and her husband Tirtha Roy. Suprna, a long-time patient, had found solace in his medicine, but lately, she had been plagued by a new set of problems. Breathing difficulties and lung issues had become a daily struggle for her, while even Tirtha, the Superintendent of Police, was experiencing mild breathing problems during his commute to the SP office.

Suprna Roy : (weakly) Thank you, Neem Baba. Your medicine brings me relief like no other. The allergic attacks have been under control but last two months I have been having problems. There are breathing and lung problems. The air seemed to be very heavy. My husband Tirtha Roy is also facing mild breathing problems while travelling to the SP office to join his duty.

The influx of patients seeking Neem Baba's help with lung problems had caught his attention, and he couldn't help but ponder the reasons behind this sudden surge. The sheer number of people reporting lung problems was alarming. Day after day, a large number of individuals would come to him, all with similar symptoms. Neem Baba's concern deepened, and he began to question the air quality in Burdwan.

As he looked around, his ashram nestled near the Sithala Temple, he marveled at the neem forest-like environment that enveloped the area. All the Neem Trees were full of Neem flowers as if grace was flowing in the entire ashram. The air here had always felt pure and refreshing, providing a sense of rejuvenation. But what about the air beyond these sacred grounds? Had the general air quality in East-Burdwan become contaminated? Why was there so much of a hit? The temperature crossed the mark of 45 and there was no rain. Was there something amiss, an unseen force affecting the health of the people?

The thought of a new variant of COVID-19 crossed his mind. The pandemic had wreaked havoc across the world, and new mutations were a constant concern. Could it be that a different strain was causing these respiratory issues? Neem Baba couldn't ignore the possibility, as the symptoms bore similarities to those associated with airborne diseases.

Neem Baba: "After returning to Burdwan there are many people who are coming to me and stating that they are having lung problems. Every day it is hundreds of people are coming stating the same kind of Symptoms. Is there something wrong with the Air? The Sithala Temple has a Neem Forest-like environment with Neem flowers all around so I hope this air is very pure. But is it that generally with Burdwan? Is the Air contaminated? Why there are so many patients with airborne disease? Is it a new variant of Covid?

Deep in thought, Neem Baba contemplated the situation. He had always been attuned to the well-being of his devotees and the community around him. Their health was intertwined with his spiritual journey. His concern for Suprna and Tirtha, and the multitude of patients seeking his guidance, fueled his determination to uncover the truth.

Neem Baba wanted to delve into the depths of this mysterious influx of lung-related cases. He wanted to investigate the air quality in Burdwan, seeking answers from experts, analyzing data, and raising awareness about the importance of clean air and its impact on human health. He always wanted his ashram would become a center for research and healing, not just for the soul but also for the physical well-being of those who sought refuge within its walls. But where is Dr. Gopal? Dr. Gopal has not come to visit his Ashram since he came back. He can be a great help in finding the real cause of this sudden surge in lung cases.

As Neem Baba continued his quest for solutions, the town of East Burdwan remained a serene backdrop, seemingly untouched by the storm brewing nearby. The narrow lanes and ancient buildings whispered tales of a cherished history, a testament to the deep roots that bound the community together.

The tranquility of East Burdwan, where time moved at a leisurely pace, stood in stark contrast to the impending threat posed by Satyananda

Adani and his ambitious project. The news of the Elysian campus and its chemical factories sent ripples of anticipation and anxiety through the town. The people, rooted in their love for their homeland, instinctively sensed the potential cost of this so-called progress.

Chapter 6: Threat in Sanjeeveni

20th April, 2024. (Saturday) Sanjeeveni Multispeciality Hospital

Dr. Gopal Subhramaniam the CMD of Sanjeeveni Multispeciality Hospital stood in his office, his face reflecting a mixture of concern and determination. The words of Arnab, the marketing chief, and Suhasini Mitra, the Head of the Burdwan Hospital Unit, echoed in his mind, each syllable painting a vivid picture of impending doom. The boardroom chamber of Sanjeevani Multispeciality Hospital was a place of authority and decision-making, but today it has transformed into a sanctuary of uncertainty and fear. Dr. Gopal's troubled pacing echoed through the room, the tension palpable in his every step. The walls seemed to close in on them, suffocating them with the weight of impending doom. The air grew heavy with silence as Arnab and Suhasini exchanged nervous glances. The gravity of their findings weighed on them, each word spoken amplifying the sense of unease that filled the chamber. The once pristine space now felt suffused with an invisible darkness, casting long shadows across their faces.

Dr. Gopal: (paces back and forth, troubled) Arnab, Suhasini, what you've just told me... it's truly unsettling. Are you certain about this information Dr Abir and Dr Moumita?

Arnab: (nervously) Dr. Gopal, I assure you, the data Dr Abir and Dr Moumita have gathered is accurate. Adani's project Pesticide factory is emitting a poisonous gas Sulphur Oxide and Sulphur Tri-oxide and PM2.5 and PM10 are rising in alarming levels and it's spreading rapidly towards our hospital and the Sitala Temple. At the same time, they have stocked large quantities of Methyl Isocyanate. That produces Pesticides and now with temperature rising about 45 centigrade and IMD giving red alerts this gas chamber could burst. Methyl Isocyanate is highly combustible and it spreads in the air very fast. Over to that due to the intense heat, there is a Temperature inversion. This means the hot air remains close to the ground and it cannot due to vertical mixing and cold air remains above. The pollutants can be locked and the intensity of pollutants in particular places around the campus can be fatal for anybody who is even traveling on the roads near campus. This is a dire situation in how climate change can affect air pollution.

Suhasini: (with concern) Yes, Dr. Gopal. The gas poses a grave threat to the environment and the health of our patients and staff. We cannot ignore this imminent danger.

Outside the grand windows, the sun dipped below the horizon, casting a glow on the surrounding landscape. The flickering lights of the town below seemed to mirror the uncertainty that gripped their hearts. The future, once filled with promise and hope, now appeared shrouded in a foreboding mist.

Dr. Gopal's voice broke the silence, his tone filled with a mix of determination and desperation. His words reverberated off the walls, reflecting the magnitude of the task that lay before them. But even as he spoke, a nagging doubt lingered in the back of his mind. Would their efforts be enough? Could they truly overcome the powerful forces that threatened to tear their world apart?

Dr. Gopal: (clenching his fists) This is unimaginable! Sanjeevini Multispeciality Hospital and the Sitala Temple are not just structures.

They hold deep significance for our town. We cannot let them be destroyed.

Arnab's fidgeting fingers betrayed his anxiety as he leaned closer, his voice barely above a whisper. The realization that their fight might attract dangerous attention sent chills down their spines. The very thought of facing powerful entities who lurked in the shadows sent shivers through the room as if the walls themselves trembled in anticipation.

Arnab: (whispering) There's something even more disturbing, Dr. Gopal. Adani's project seems to have the support of powerful entities. They might try to suppress our concerns.

Suhasini's unwavering determination pierced through the gloom, her words cutting through the stifling atmosphere. Her resolute spirit injected a glimmer of hope, offering a beacon of light amidst the encroaching darkness. But as she spoke, her eyes flickered with an unspoken question: Were they prepared for the sacrifices that lay ahead?

Suhasini: (determined) We cannot allow that to happen,

Arnab: (looking over his shoulder) Dr. Gopal, we need to be cautious. These are dangerous times. The Green cover that used to shade Burdwan is destroyed in the name of development, widening roads, and building skyscrapers. This year we have experienced temperatures above 45 degrees which is the highest in the last 40 years. And then you have this poisonous gas. The truth might expose us to unforeseen risks. The people need to understand that health and the environment are interlinked. You can't be healthy in an environmentally hazardous situation. But do we have the power to explain that to people?

Suhasini: (resolute) We understand the risks, Arnab, but justice and the welfare of our community are at stake. We cannot afford to back down. We must find allies who share our cause and expose the sinister nature of Adani's project.

Dr. Gopal's clenched fists punctuated his resolve as if he were physically gathering the strength to face the storm that loomed on the horizon. The weight of responsibility settled upon his shoulders, threatening to crush him under its burden. But he refused to falter. The fire in his eyes mirrored the flickering determination that burned within each of them.

Dr. Gopal. We must protect the lives entrusted to us and the sacredness of our land. We have to take action before it's too late. (pausing, his eyes blazing) You're right Suhasini. We cannot sit idly by while our beloved hospital and temple face destruction. We need to gather evidence, rally the townspeople, and make our voices heard.

Dr. Gopal: (firmly) In this difficult the only hope is Neem Baba has returned from Rishikesh. Neem Baba has always been a pillar of wisdom and guidance. We need his support to awaken the people and unite them against this threat. Together, we can make a difference.

Time, their most precious resource, seemed to slip away as Arnab's watch ticked relentlessly. With every passing second, Adani's project inched closer, like a shadowy specter inching its way toward their haven. They could not afford to delay any longer; action was their only hope in the face of impending disaster.

Arnab: (looking at his watch) Time is of the essence,

Dr. Gopal. Adani's project is advancing rapidly. We need to act swiftly and decisively.

Taking a deep breath, Suhasini exhaled slowly, channeling her inner strength. She acknowledged the risks, yet she also recognized that retreating meant surrendering their town to a future marred by darkness and destruction. The weight of their mission settled upon her like armor, emboldening her resolve.

Suhasini: (taking a deep breath) Dr. Gopal, with your leadership and our unwavering determination, we will overcome this ordeal. We will protect our hospital, the temple, and the very soul of our town.

Dr. Gopal's gaze met theirs, their collective determination intertwining in an unspoken agreement. In that moment, the boardroom chamber became a sanctuary of resilience and defiance. They were prepared to defy the odds, to challenge the powerful forces that threatened their existence.

Dr. Gopal: (looking at both of them, a steely resolve in his eyes) Let's begin our fight, my friends. We will gather evidence, mobilize the townspeople, and expose the truth. No matter the risks, we will not rest until justice is served and our cherished land is safe once more.

As they left the chamber, the door closed behind them with a soft thud, sealing their resolve within its confines. Outside, the world awaited, its future uncertain, but with the shared commitment of Dr. Gopal, Arnab, Suhasini, Dr Abir, and Dr Moumita there remained a flicker of hope—a spark of light amidst the encroaching darkness.

Sanjeevini Multispeciality Hospital, the very institution Dr. Gopal had dedicated his life, was under threat. But it wasn't just the hospital; it was something much more profound and sacred that hung in the balance.

With their commitment to justice, the stage was set for a battle that would transcend the physical realm. As the three of them stood together, their collective resolve reverberated in the air. The battle against Adani's project had just begun, and the suspense and thrill of their mission filled the room, leaving no doubt that they were prepared to go to extraordinary lengths to protect what they held   dear.

******

East Burdwan, a vibrant town nestled amidst rolling hills and lush greenery, was known for its close-knit community and the presence of Sanjeevani Multispeciality Hospital. The hospital stood as a beacon of hope, providing exceptional healthcare to the town's residents and those in neighboring areas.

But beyond the idyllic façade, a storm was brewing. The Adani Corporation had set its sights on Burdwan and has established its ambitious Elysium project—a colossal endeavor that promised innovation and progress. However, whispers of concern had spread through the town, fueled by rumors of the project's potential environmental impact and the consequences it could have on the cherished Sitala Temple, a spiritual sanctuary revered by the locals.

Within the confines of the hospital's boardroom, Arnab, a key member of the hospital's marketing team, found himself at the center of an intricate web of secrets and temptation.

Arnab: (answers the call, cautiously) Hello?

Unknown Caller: Good evening, Mr. Arnab. I hope I'm not disturbing you.

Arnab: (curious) No, not at all. May I know who's calling?

Unknown Caller: My name is Priya, and I'm the HR Head of Adani's Elysium project in Burdwan.

Arnab: (surprised) Oh, I see. How can I help you, Priya?

Priya: Well, Arnab, I've been observing your work at Sanjeevani Multispeciality Hospital, and I must say, you're quite impressive.

Arnab: (flattered) Thank you, Priya. I appreciate your kind words.

Priya: I'll get straight to the point, Arnab. We have a proposition for you—a lucrative offer that you might find hard to resist.

Arnab: (intrigued) Go on, Priya. What is this offer?

Priya: We are aware of your concerns regarding the Adani project, and we believe that your expertise and knowledge could be of great value to us. We are prepared to pay you double your current salary, with the money directly transferred to your bank account. In return, we simply ask for regular updates on any steps taken by Sanjeevani Multispeciality Hospital against Adani's projects.

Arnab: (taken aback) Wait, are you asking me to act as a spy? To report on my organization

The call he had just received from Priya, the enigmatic HR Head of Adani's Elysium project, had introduced a clandestine offer—an offer that tested his loyalty and moral compass.

As Arnab stood there, contemplating the choices before him, the room itself seemed to reflect the mounting tension. The walls, adorned with framed accolades and photographs of the hospital's dedicated staff, now felt oppressive, as if they held secrets waiting to be unraveled. The mahogany table, once a symbol of collaboration and progress, now stood as a divide between duty and personal gain.

Arnab: (conflicted) This is a lot to take in, Priya. I never expected such an offer. But isn't this unethical? Betraying my colleagues and the hospital?

Priya: (softly) Arnab, think of your future, your dreams. This is an opportunity that may never come again. We won't ask you to compromise your safety. Your role as our informant will remain discreet, and no one will ever know.

Arnab: (hesitant) I understand the lure of such an offer, Priya. But this feels like playing with fire. What if I'm caught? What if my conscience eats away at me?

Priya: (slyly) That's a risk you'll have to weigh, Arnab. Only you can decide what truly matters to you. We believe in your potential and your hunger for success. This is your chance to make an impact on a grand scale.

Outside the boardroom windows, the town's landscape painted a contrasting picture. The sun cast long shadows over the sprawling Elysium project, its construction echoing a sense of impending transformation. The streets, once bustling with the familiar faces of townspeople, now seemed hushed, as if nature itself held its breath, waiting for the storm to break.

Arnab's mind raced, torn between the promise of a prosperous future and the weight of his responsibilities. The thought of doubling his salary and ascending the corporate ladder was undeniably enticing. It spoke to the aspirations he held deep within his heart—a chance to make a mark, to forge his destiny. But the cost was steep, and the betrayal of his colleagues and the hospital weighed heavily on his conscience.

The echoes of Priya's voice lingered, the very essence of suspense and thrill hanging in the air. The shadows danced across the room as if toying with Arnab's indecision. The fate of Sanjeevani Multispeciality Hospital and the sanctity of the Sitala Temple seemed to hinge on his choice—a choice that could either expose the true intentions of the Adani Corporation or plunge him into a world of secrecy and manipulation.

At that moment, Arnab realized that his decision extended beyond his desires. It held the power to shape the future of the entire community, safeguard their well-being, and preserve their sacred traditions. The suspenseful weight of his choice pressed upon him, urging him to tread carefully and uncover the truth hidden beneath the surface.

As the minutes ticked away where Arnab and Priya both silently contemplated each other's thoughts, Arnab knew that he could not face this challenge alone. The stage was set for a battle that transcended personal gain—an intricate dance of suspense and thrill that would test his mettle and call upon the strength of the entire hospital team.

With determination etched upon his face, Arnab took a deep breath, resolved to navigate the treacherous path that lay ahead. The fate of Sanjeevani Multispeciality Hospital, the Sitala Temple, and the very essence of East Burdwan itself hung in the balance, and Arnab was determined to unravel the mysteries that threatened their existence.

Priya: (softening her tone) Take your time, Arnab. But remember, opportunities like this don't come knocking twice. We await your decision eagerly. Can we meet somewhere?

As the call ended, Arnab gave the concluding response "I will let you know Priya", Arnab stared at his phone, a mix of emotions washing over him. He quickly typed Priya + Adani Corporation and the result shocked him when he found on LinkedIn that the HR head of Adani Corporation is none other than Priya Adani – the youngest daughter of Satyananda Adani. The temptation of wealth and power tugged at his ambitions, while the weight of loyalty and integrity burdened his conscience. The room around him seemed to close in as if he were trapped in a moral dilemma, unsure of which path to choose.

Arnab knew that the offer held great allure, but he also recognized the potential consequences of his actions. Would he succumb to the greed that was being used against him, or would he remain true to his principles and the values that had guided him thus far? Only time would reveal the choice he would ultimately make—a choice that could shape not only his destiny but also the fate of Sanjeevani Multispeciality Hospital.

NEEM BABA RETURNS

Chapter 6: Dr Gopal meets Neem Baba

21ʰ April, 2024. (Sunday) Sinthala Temple

The scene shifted from the internal struggle of Arnab to the determined resolve of Neem Baba and Dr. Gopal. As the weight of their responsibilities settled upon them, their paths intertwined, converging in a shared purpose that would redefine their roles in the battle against adversity. For a year, Neem Baba has been out of reach as he went for his spiritual regeneration retreat in Rishikesh. Dr Gopal will sometimes feel directionless without the presence of his master who has guided him in every phase of life. Neem Baba, his presence emanating wisdom and serenity, stood alongside Dr. Gopal all the impending challenges he has faced in his life.

Dr. Gopal, still grappling with a sense of disbelief, found himself trapped in a nightmarish reality. The once-promising name of Adani had transformed into a symbol of fear and uncertainty. He felt powerless even owning one of the most powerful groups of Hospitals in India, in comparison to Adani, who was one the Forbes richest people living in India. Still, like a toxic gas permeating the air, their project loomed as a lethal threat to everything they held dear—the environment, the people, and the very essence of their town.

But Neem Baba's presence has always served as a beacon of hope. His unwavering belief in the power of resistance and the strength of community has galvanized Dr. Gopal's spirit earlier too.

Dr. Gopal Subhramaniam, a concerned advocate for public health and the environment, stood before an imaginary audience, his frustration evident in his voice and demeanor. The last year had been nothing short of critical for East Burdwan, as the very fabric of its environment and the well-being of its inhabitants deteriorated day by day.

The destruction of green shades, once abundant and refreshing, had left a barren landscape in its wake. The rising temperatures surpassed tolerable limits, rendering numerous patients victims of heat strokes, seeking solace in his hospital. Dr. Gopal tirelessly emphasized these issues in every public meeting, hoping to ignite a spark of awareness and action.

However, it seemed that the authorities and political masters were preoccupied with trivial matters, indulging in the superficialities of arranging football matches or hosting glamorous actresses. Their priorities had become misplaced, as they chased after fleeting moments of mass publicity and engaged in petty battles for votes.

Dr. Gopal couldn't fathom how the very individuals entrusted with the well-being of the masses could disregard matters of public health and the environment. The roads, once pathways for progress, were now adorned with towering posters, proudly proclaiming achievements and projects that had never seen the light of day.

This state of affairs simply could not continue. Dr. Gopal recognized the urgency of the situation and the need for intervention. With Neem Baba's absence, the past year has witnessed a steady decline in the health and environmental conditions of East Burdwan. He longed for his revered master's return, throughout the year for the guiding light and influence that Neem Baba had wielded in uplifting the masses.

Dr. Gopal's heart ached for the town he held dear, for its people who suffered due to the negligence of those in power. He yearned for a renewed sense of purpose, for the reinstatement of a collective drive to restore the environment and prioritize public health. The time had come for action, for the authorities and political masters to be held accountable for their inaction and neglect.

Dr. Gopal's voice carried a mixture of frustration, determination, and longing. He called upon the higher powers to recognize the urgency of the situation, to step away from trivialities, and to refocus their efforts on the upliftment of the masses. East Burdwan's health and environment hung in the balance, awaiting the action of Neem Baba and the rekindling of hope for a better future. Today he was delighted that after a year Neem Baba wanted to meet him and called him in his ashram in Sitala Temple.

He imagined in mind with renewed determination, they would rally the townspeople, ignite the flames of resistance, and stand united against the encroachment upon their cherished land.

Dr. Gopal would redefine their roles as leaders, guiding the townspeople on a path of defiance against the forces that sought to exploit and destroy. The destiny of Sanjeevani Multispeciality Hospital and the very essence of their town hung in the balance, their actions carrying the potential to shape the future for generations to come.

And so, with a shared purpose and hearts brimming with resolve, Dr. Gopal prepared to lead the charge. The battle against the encroachment had just begun, and they would harness the collective strength of the townspeople, their voices rising in unison against the looming threat. In this pivotal moment, their conviction and unwavering determination would serve as a testament to the power of resistance and the enduring spirit of a community united.

Yet Dr. Gopal couldn't help but feel a sense of disbelief as if trapped in a nightmare he couldn't wake up from. Adani's project, the very name that had once held promise and progress, now brought only fear and uncertainty. It seemed they were emitting poisonous gas, a lethal threat to the environment, the people, and everything that held meaning in this town.

The gravity of the situation weighed heavily upon Dr. Gopal's shoulders. The multispeciality hospital, a beacon of hope and healing for countless lives, now faced an uncertain future. And to add to the mounting calamity, the beloved Sitala Temple, a symbol of faith and solace, also found itself in the crosshairs of this insidious project.

Dr. Gopal knew that relocation was not merely an inconvenience but a loss that would forever scar the town's soul. The hospital's very essence was intertwined with the land it stood upon, and the temple held a spiritual significance that couldn't be replicated elsewhere.

He knew he had to act swiftly and decisively. Driven by a resolute determination, he reached out to Neem Baba, the spiritual guide who had a deep understanding of the interconnectedness between man, nature, and the divine.

The battle that lay ahead would test their strength, resilience, and faith. It would demand sacrifices and unwavering courage. But Dr. Gopal, along with Neem Baba and the townspeople, would not yield. They would fight tooth and nail, using every means at their disposal to ensure justice was served, the poisonous gas ceased, and their precious land was safeguarded.

As he prepared to face the challenges ahead, Dr. Gopal steeled himself, knowing that the battle was not just about a hospital or a temple. It was about the values they held dear, the spirit of unity, and the indomitable human will to protect what was right.

With that fiery determination burning within him, Dr. Gopal stepped out of his office, ready to face the storm head-on. The battle for Sanjeevini

Multispeciality Hospital and the Sitala Temple had begun, and the suspense and thrill of this fight would leave an indelible mark on the lives of all those involved.

As Neem Baba and Dr. Gopal Subharamaniam engaged in conversation within the peaceful confines of the Sitala Mandir, their voices carried determination and hope after Suhasini Mitra and Arnab gave a report detailing the threats and challenges Adani's project brought to East Burdwan Health City.

They understood the challenges ahead, but they also knew the strength that lay in unity. Their shared resolve to protect East Burdwan from the clutches of corporate greed sparked a flame of defiance in their hearts.

With their commitment to justice, the stage was set for a battle that would transcend the physical realm. Neem Baba and Dr. Gopal

Subharamaniam would lead the charge, rallying the townspeople, and igniting a spirit of resistance against the encroachment upon their cherished land.

The tranquil air of Sitala Mandir and the historical beauty of East Burdwan stood as reminders of the resilience and spirit of a community ready to defend its home. As they embarked on this arduous journey, the legacy of Burdwan and the healing powers of Neem Baba would collide with the relentless forces of destruction, giving rise to an epic battle that would test the mettle of their resolve and shape the destiny of the town they held dear.

Dr. Gopal: (entering the chamber, concerned) Neem Baba, something ominous is happening in Burdwan. This massive Chemical factory project by Satyananda Adani is emitting poisonous Sulphuric acid and Sulphur Trioxide invading the full campus. It's bound to disrupt the tranquility of our town. The researchers of our multispecialty hospital have done a study and this poisonous gas will both harm the people coming into our hospital and Sitala Mandir. Besides it will raise the PM2.5 and PM10 figures to an alarming level.

Neem Baba: (raising an eyebrow) Adani? The same tycoon who seeks profit above all else? This doesn't bode well for Burdwan, I fear.

Dr. Gopal: (nodding) Yes, his multicrore project threatens to bring chaos and destruction. The historical town we know and love will never be the same.

Neem Baba: (placing a hand on Dr. Gopal's shoulder) We must remain vigilant, and make the media vigilant too Gopal. Why don't you make the report public? Sambaran can help you with this, he is a good reporter. He has to make people aware and we have to heal, to protect the well-being of our people and this sacred land.

Dr. Gopal: But what can we do, Neem Baba? Making the report public will do nothing, Adani is influential and seemingly untouchable. He will put a defamation against us.

Neem Baba: (smiling determinedly) Remember, my student, environmental disaster shall not be treated so lightly. There is a separate Tribunal for environmental law violation – NGT and you know that very well. I think media is the fourth pillar of democracy and they have the strength to unite people for a cause. After the media report comes up we shall rally the people, and raise our voices against this onslaught. Together, we can make a difference. A movement against this should be started to stop the poisoning of air.

Dr. Gopal: (inspired) You're right, Neem Baba. We should start a new public space where people can come together to protest it. We won't let corporate greed destroy what is precious to us. We'll fight for the tranquility and harmony of East Burdwan.

Neem Baba: (placing a hand on Dr. Gopal's other shoulder) That's the spirit, Gopal. Let our actions speak louder than their greed. We shall protect our town, our people, and the legacy that East Burdwan holds.

Together, Neem Baba and Dr. Gopal stand united, ready to confront the impending storm brought by Satyananda Adani's project, determined to preserve the serenity of East Burdwan and bring about justice.

Chapter 7: The Environmental Disaster Unveiled

22nd April, 2024. (Monday) Canteen of Sanjeevani Multispeciality Hospital

In the bustling canteen of Sanjeevani Multispeciality Hospital, located near the revered Sitala Mandir, a symphony of voices filled the air. Patients from various walks of life had gathered around tables, their conversations punctuated by the clinking of cutlery and the tantalizing aroma of hospital food. The atmosphere crackled with a unique blend of anxiety and fear, their faces etched with the distress caused by the deteriorating air quality in their beloved town of East Burdwan.

It was the report published by Investigate Journalist Sambaran Roy in the Burdwan Daily, that had exposed the dire situation. The patients exchanged concerned glances, their eyes mirroring the weight of their shared experiences.

Ravi, a middle-aged man with lines etched deeply on his weary face, vented his frustration. His voice trembled with anger as he exclaimed, "Did you see the smoke from that Chemical factory of Adani? It's choking the air! It feels like we're suffocating."

Tiya, a young woman gripping an inhaler tightly in her hand, nodded in agreement, her eyes filled with concern. "Yes, it's unbearable! I can hardly breathe. This pollution has reached dangerous levels. How did it come to this?"

Sanjay, a senior citizen struggling to catch his breath, joined the conversation with a somber tone. "And look at the Baka River! It's covered in a thick layer of smoke. It's devastating! Our town is drowning in toxic fumes."

Meera, a woman in her forties, her forehead etched with worry lines, chimed in, her voice laden with frustration. "This is all happening because of that Chemical factory project. They didn't consider the environmental impact at all. They've unleashed this catastrophe upon us."

The canteen hummed with a sense of shared outrage. Ravi's eyes flashed with anger as he continued, "Exactly! They destroyed so many trees during the construction. Now we're paying the price with tremendous heat and toxic air. Our health is at stake."

Tiya, her inhaler pressed to her lips, added, "It's affecting everyone's health. Neem Baba must be overwhelmed with patients suffering from respiratory problems. We need his guidance and healing."

Sanjay, his voice strained from labored breathing, expressed his disappointment. "I heard he's been working tirelessly to help people, but there are just too many cases for him to handle alone. We need more support."

Meera, her voice tinged with frustration, stated firmly, "It's a shame the local administration seems clueless about the situation. They should have anticipated these issues and protected our town."

Determined to make a change, Ravi clenched his fists and spoke with conviction. "We need to raise awareness and demand action. Our town is being destroyed by this greed and negligence. We can't stay silent anymore."

Tiya, her eyes filled with determination, echoed his sentiment. "We must unite and fight for our health and the health of future generations. This cannot go on. We need to protect our town."

Sanjay, his voice filled with resolve, nodded in agreement. "I agree. We need to make our voices heard and hold those responsible accountable for their actions. We can't let them get away with this."

Meera, her gaze unwavering, concluded with determination, "Let's gather more people, organize protests, and bring attention to the plight of East Burdwan. Together, we can stand up against this destruction and fight for a healthier future."

As their voices grew louder, drowning out the clattering of dishes, the patients in the canteen made an unspoken pact. They understood that their collective strength could bring about change, not just for their well-being, but for the well-being of their town and the generations yet to come. The seed of resistance had been planted, and the fight for clean air and a sustainable future had begun in the heart of the hospital's bustling canteen.

At about a six-foot distance, Superintendent of Police, Tirtha Roy sat with his wife in the humble cafeteria of Sanjeevani Multispeciality Hospital. Clad in ordinary attire, he concealed his true identity as a man entrusted with upholding the law.

(Tirtha Roy appears like an ordinary person, not revealing his identity as the Superintendent of Police. His mind is preoccupied with the recent order he received from the commissioner, relating to the arrest of investigative journalist Sambaran Roy for defaming Satyananda Adani and his Adani Corporation. Tirtha overhears conversations about Sambaran's report in the Burdwan Daily, which has caused unrest and widespread discussions in public places.)

As he consumed his meal, the weight of a recent order from the commissioner of police hung heavily upon him. This directive called for the arrest of investigative journalist Sambaran Roy, accused of defaming Satyananda Adani and his Adani Corporation. Tirtha, however, found himself grappling with a moral dilemma that threatened to engulf his thoughts.

Tirtha Roy: (sighs deeply, speaking to himself) These are trying times indeed. As a Superintendent of Police, I have to enforce the orders given to me by the commissioner, but this particular order has put me in an immense dilemma.

Whispers of Sambaran's report in the Burdwan Daily had permeated the air, causing unrest and igniting discussions among the townspeople. The photographs captured by Tillotama had stirred a storm, casting doubt upon the credibility of Adani and his corporation. Tirtha's concern deepened as he contemplated the potential environmental hazards associated with their activities.

(Tirtha glances at his wife, his face filled with worry. He struggles to balance his commitment to upholding the law and his growing concerns about the potential environmental hazards caused by Adani's activities.)

Tirtha Roy: (whispering) The report by Sambaran Roy, those photographs by Tillotama... they have stirred up a storm in our city. Satyananda Adani's anger is understandable, as it has tarnished his reputation and that of his corporation. But are these allegations truly baseless?

(Tirtha's mind races, torn between the orders he has received and the information he obtained from Neem Baba regarding the sudden increase in lung-related cases after the opening of the factory. He contemplates the political influence that shields Adani from scrutiny.)

Within the confines of his mind, conflicting forces battled for supremacy. On one side stood his duty as a law enforcement officer, bound to fulfill the orders bestowed upon him. On the other side grew his mounting worries, fueled by the information he had received from Neem Baba. The sudden increase in lung-related cases following the factory's opening painted a disturbing picture, one that raised questions about the administration's unwillingness to challenge Adani's power.

Tirtha Roy: (muttering, conflicted) The district administration, the media, and the political masters are all turning a blind eye to the potential environmental hazard... all because Adani has poured immense funds into their pockets. Is it right to prioritize one man's reputation over the safety and well-being of so many lives?

(Tirtha's hands clench into fists as he weighs the consequences of his actions. He knows that arresting Sambaran Roy will silence his voice and suppress the truth that could protect the people of East Burdwan.)

As he muttered to himself, Tirtha questioned the ethics of prioritizing one man's reputation over the well-being and safety of countless lives. The district administration, media, and political powers appeared entangled in a web woven by Adani's generous financial contributions. The weight of this realization pressed upon Tirtha's conscience, leaving him torn between duty and the greater good.

But a flicker of determination ignited within him. He clutched his fists, his resolve solidifying with each passing moment. In that crowded cafeteria, he made a silent vow to himself and the people of Burdwan. No longer would he be a mere puppet, dancing to the tunes of those who placed self-interest above the welfare of the community.

Tirtha's eyes darted around, ensuring that his words remained unheard by prying ears. He affirmed his commitment to undertake a thorough investigation, to gather evidence that would shine a light on the truth. Justice and the safety of the people would guide his every action. He understood that the path he had chosen would be fraught with challenges, but he embraced them with unwavering determination.

Tirtha Roy: (determined) But I took an oath to serve and protect. My duty lies in upholding the law, not in compromising the lives of innocent citizens. If there is even a slight chance that these allegations hold truth, I cannot turn a blind eye.

(Tirtha looks around, ensuring no one is eavesdropping. His voice grows resolute as he makes a silent promise to himself and the people of East Burdwan.)

Tirtha Roy: (whispering, determined) I will not be a puppet to those in power who prioritize their interests over the welfare of our community. I will investigate this matter thoroughly, gather evidence, and make a decision that aligns with justice and the safety of our people. The truth must prevail, no matter the challenges it brings.

As his gaze shifted towards his wife, a mixture of determination and concern swirled in his eyes. The lunch continued, now infused with a newfound purpose. Tirtha understood that his decision had set him on a treacherous journey, but he remained steadfast in his commitment to do what was right, even if it meant standing against the powerful forces that sought to silence the truth.

(Tirtha glances at his wife, a mix of determination and concern in his eyes. With newfound purpose, he continues his lunch, knowing that the path he has chosen will be fraught with obstacles, but steadfast in his commitment to do what is right.)

Chapter 8: Unveiling the Truth

23rd April, 2024. (Tuesday) Sinthala Temple

Sambaran Roy, a sprawling metropolis nestled amidst towering skyscrapers and bustling streets, the campus of Elysium thrived as a hub of technological advancements and corporate power. However, beneath its gleaming exterior, a deep-rooted issue and unhappiness festered, threatening the very essence of its existence and bringing irony to the meaning of the name.

The Health city's serene outskirts housed a magnificent landscape of lush forests, which has a Sanjeevini multispeciality hospital on one side and the Sitala temple on the other side. It was here that Adani Corporation had erected its colossal pesticide factory, the heart of their agro-allied industrial empire. But unseen by the masses, this beacon of progress hid a dark secret that would soon unravel.

Investigative reporter Sambaran Roy had dedicated his life to unearthing truths hidden from the public eye. With unwavering determination and an unyielding pursuit of justice, he delved into the activities of Adani's new factory. His relentless investigations led him to a disturbing revelation—the smoke belching from the Pesticide factory's towering chimneys had become a malevolent force, poisoning the air with a high degree of PM2.5 and PM10 along with Sulphur dioxide and Sulphur Trioxide, and devastating the environment. It has also a large repository of a fatal gas used for producing Pesticides – Menthayl Isocynate. Is this gas the real reason for the death of Dr Rahul Maitra and the fisherman community slums? But how Sanjeevani Multispeciality Hospital and Sithala Temple could save themselves from the gaseous dissemination.

Sambaran had earlier targeted Neem Baba as the major suspect in Dr. Rahul Maitra's enmity towards Neem Baba.

However, then the pesticide factory and its gas emissions went into Sambaran knowledge. But Sambaran is still in doubt. Though Sambaran feels quite comfortable with doubt as it reveals new knowledge to him. Sambaran's findings struck a nerve within the citizens of East Burdwan and also with the corridors of power, shaking the foundations of the influential Adani conglomerate. Recognizing the imminent threat to their reputation and financial interests, Adani swiftly executed their countermove, leveraging their immense influence to orchestrate Sambaran's arrest. The truth became a hostage to their power.

However, in the city's outskirts, a revered figure Neem Baba dwelled in his tranquil ashram in

Sitala Temple. His profound wisdom, spiritual enlightenment, and unwavering commitment to justice made him a beacon of hope for those seeking solace and guidance. Hearing of Sambaran's plight, Neem Baba faced a dilemma between right and wrong and sensed an opportunity to restore balance and protect the delicate equilibrium between humanity and nature.

In the depths of his tranquil ashram, Neem Baba's heart brims with a mix of awe and sorrow. The wonder of divine actions unfolds before his eyes, revealing the painful truth of Sambaran Roy's plight. How can it be that a righteous and truthful conscience keeper, a guardian of society like Sambaran, is punished and tortured by the relentless power of greedy individuals like Adani?

"In the sacred stillness of my ashram, I ponder upon the delicate dance between truth and power that unfolds in the world around us. The arrest of Sambaran, the investigative journalist who dared to shine a light on Adani's deeds, weighs heavily on my conscience. As a spiritual being, should I step forward and become directly involved in his case? Is it my place to wield the sword of justice in this mortal realm?"

Neem Baba gazes out at the serene beauty of the natural world, seeking solace in its wisdom. The gentle breeze rustles the leaves, whispering secrets of resilience and endurance. The sun casts its golden rays, illuminating the path of righteousness that Sambaran had embarked upon, only to be met with darkness and persecution.

"The truth is a fragile entity, easily held captive by those who seek to protect their reputation and wealth. Adani, with their vast influence and resources, has maneuvered skillfully, ensnaring the truth in the shackles of their power. But I, Neem Baba, stand at the crossroads, torn between my spiritual duty and the call of justice."

As a spiritual being, I have to protect and nurture this fragile balance. But can I do so from the confines of my ashram, offering solace and guidance to those who seek it? Or is there a higher calling, a path that demands direct action to restore justice and heal the wounds inflicted upon our beloved Earth?

"Sambaran's plight resonates deeply within me, for it is a battle fought not only in the realms of law and politics but also in the sacred realm of nature. The harmony of the universe is at stake, as the actions of Adani and their corporation endanger the delicate equilibrium between humanity and the natural world. The rivers choke with toxic fumes, the air becomes a suffocating veil, and the earth itself cries out for respite."

In my meditations, I have sought guidance from the divine, asking for clarity amidst the tumultuous currents of this world. The answer, whispers in my ear, reminding me of the teachings that have shaped my journey. It is not enough to merely observe and preach; true spirituality calls for active engagement in the pursuit of justice.

"The time has come for me, Neem Baba, to step beyond the walls of my ashram and embrace the role of a warrior for truth and harmony. The battle against Adani's greed and negligence is not fought with swords or violence but with the unwavering strength of conviction and the light of awareness."

"I shall lend my voice to the silenced, stand as a shield for the oppressed, and offer my wisdom as a guide through the treacherous path of justice. The power of Adani may be formidable, but the force of truth and unity is greater still. With the collective strength of the people, we shall break the chains that bind the truth and restore balance to our town, East Burdwan."

"I hope my disciples, will join me in this endeavor. Let us raise our voices, awaken the slumbering conscience of the administration, and ignite the flames of change. Together, we shall manifest a world where power bows to truth, where the welfare of the people and the harmony of nature prevail over greed and negligence."

"The time has come for Neem Baba to step forward, to become a beacon of hope in these tumultuous times. May the divine guide my actions, and may the spirit of justice guide us all."

The tears well in Neem Baba's eyes as he contemplates the immense weight of injustice. How can it be that those who strive to uncover the truth and protect the voiceless become victims themselves? The divine order, mysterious and unfathomable, sometimes allows the wicked to thrive and the virtuous to suffer.

Yet, amid sorrow, Neem Baba's spirit remains undeterred. He finds solace in the knowledge that the divine plan, though incomprehensible to mortal minds, is driven by a higher purpose. The struggles of Sambaran, the torment he endures, are not in vain. They serve as a clarion call for all those who cherish justice and truth.

Neem Baba, with a heavy heart, recalls his self-talk, the resolute words spoken in the depths of his contemplation. He affirms his commitment to fight alongside Sambaran, to become a beacon of hope amidst the darkness that surrounds them. The divine has chosen him, Neem Baba, to bear witness to the unyielding strength of the human spirit.

Through his tears, Neem Baba sees the transformative power that lies within suffering.

Sambaran's persecution becomes a catalyst for change, igniting the flames of resistance and awakening the slumbering conscience of the people. It is a painful reminder that the struggle for justice is not without sacrifice and that the path of righteousness is often paved with thorns.

With renewed determination, Neem Baba steps out of his ashram, his heart aflame with compassion and unwavering resolve. He joins the chorus of voices demanding justice for Sambaran, for the people of Burdwan, and for the fragile equilibrium between humanity and nature.

The journey ahead is arduous, fraught with challenges and uncertainty. But Neem Baba embraces it with open arms, guided by the divine wisdom that flows through his veins. In the face of Adani's power, he knows that unity, truth, and unwavering conviction are the weapons that shall dismantle the fortress of greed.

As the sun sets, casting an ethereal glow over the ashram, Neem Baba finds solace in the knowledge that he is not alone. The divine walks beside him, and the spirits of the virtuous, like Sambaran Roy, watch over him. Together, they will navigate the treacherous waters of injustice, upholding the torch of truth until it illuminates every dark corner and restores balance to a world ensnared by power and corruption.

Neem Baba takes a deep breath, his heart filled with love and determination. He steps forward, ready to confront the storms that lie ahead, for he knows that in the depths of suffering, the seeds of transformation are sown.

Neem Baba, clad in white robes, ventured into the office room of Sitala temple, seeking an audience with the Superintendent of Police, a figure caught amidst the clutches of power and the ethical dilemma it presented. With a calm yet determined demeanor, Neem Baba addressed the Superintendent by phone, inquiring about the reasons behind Sambaran's arrest.

Excuse me, Tirtha. I have heard about the arrest of Sambaran Roy. May I know the reason behind it?

The Superintendent, torn between his duty to uphold the law and the influence that shackled him, cautiously revealed the truth.

Sambaran Roy's allegations against Adani's factory had struck a chord, but the overpowering reach of the conglomerate had forced their hand. Sambaran's arrest became a testament to the control of power over the truth.

Superintendent of Police: Yes, indeed. But why are you so concerned Neem Baba? Sambaran Roy earlier was responsible for a scandalous interview of Dr. Rahul Maitra making some baseless allegations against you. Look how divinely punished on the night of Ramnavami, Dr Maitra he was burned in a car accident with poisonous gas found in his lungs. It was like burning the statue of Ravana. Now it's the turn of Sambaran Roy, the investigative reporter, who made some serious allegations against Adani's new Pesticide factory. He claimed that the smoke emitted by the factory caused an environmental disaster. However, due to Adani's influence and his defamation case against Burdwan Times and Sambaran Roy, we had to take him into custody. Which I also wanted to do when he has taken that interview on you but you are not in favor of it. Unfazed by the challenges, Neem Baba offered his assistance, his voice resonating with unwavering faith in justice and the pursuit of truth. He implored the Superintendent to allow him to meet Sambaran and join forces to confront this grave issue.

Neem Baba: I understand the challenges, Tirtha. But I am not Adani. But I believe in the power of justice and truth. Please allow me to meet Sambaran and offer my assistance. Perhaps together, we can find a way to address this situation.

Superintendent of Police: Well, if you have any information or evidence that could shed light on the situation, it would be helpful. But considering the circumstances, I'm afraid it won't be easy to get Sambaran released. However, my family is indebted to you Neem Baba. You have cured my wife of chronic allergy disease from food using your Neem leave-based treatment. So, I will try my best to arrange a meeting with him, with you in your Ashram.

In the secluded sanctuary of Neem Baba's ashram where he was taken accompanied by Tirtha Roy, surrounded by the serenity of nature,

Sambaran poured out the full extent of the issue. He detailed the toxic smoke that billowed from Adani's factory, polluting the air, contaminating the rivers, and ravaging the neighboring forests. He shared his meticulously gathered evidence when he was joined by Tillotama, a collection of photographs, eyewitness testimonies, and damning internal documents, which unraveled the intricate web of deception spun by Adani.

With unwavering determination, Neem Baba acknowledged the gravity of the situation. He knew that the battle to restore justice and protect the environment required a strategic and calculated approach.

Neem Baba: Sambaran, my friend, I've learned about the gravity of the situation. Please share with me the full extent of the issue.

Sambaran Roy: Neem Baba, I'm grateful that you've come to help. Adani's factory has been spewing toxic smoke into the air for months now. The nearby rivers and forests have been severely affected, causing an environmental disaster. I gathered evidence and exposed the truth, but Adani's immense influence led to my arrest. They tried to silence me.

Neem Baba: The truth must prevail, Sambaran. We cannot let powerful interests suppress the voice of justice. We shall work together to bring light to this issue and restore balance to the environment. What evidence do you have to show when you are placed in District Court on Monday?

Sambaran Roy: I have photographs, eyewitness testimonies, and even some internal documents that prove the link between the factory's emissions and the environmental damage and I have submitted them to all my lawyers. But without the support of the authorities, it's been challenging to make a significant impact because, with the kind of money Adani has, it is obvious that if he can get me arrested on a defamation case under IPC Section 500 he can buy my lawyer too.

Neem Baba: Fear not, my friend. I have a very genuine disciple who is also a member of the Trust Board and is a lawyer specializing in the National Green Tribunal. We shall shift the case from the District Court to the National Green Tribunal where you can put a more solid presentation on how the environmental laws are violated. It can also happen that if the report is republished in any of the leading dailies of Bengal then NGT can take a Suo moto motion and then also we will get justice. I am confident he is the best lawyer to get the logistics and legal issues sorted and I am sure he shall find a way to make your voice heard and seek justice for the affected environment. Your release from custody by him will be only the beginning. Together, we will bring about the change that is needed.

Together, they devised a plan to compile their evidence and expose Adani's wrongdoing to the world. Neem Baba, wielding his influence and the power of public opinion, pledged to ensure the truth reached every corner of the city.

Neem Baba: Sambaran, we must gather all the evidence we have and present it to the public. We need to raise awareness about the environmental disaster caused by Adani's factory. I will use my influence to ensure the truth reaches the masses.

Sambaran Roy: That's a brilliant plan, Neem Baba. The more people become aware, the stronger our case will become. Let's compile all the evidence of poisonous gasses emitted and prepare a comprehensive report to expose Adani's wrongdoing and start some form of Grass root activism.

Neem Baba: Indeed, Sambaran. We must be meticulous in our approach and try to work out a plan for how we can peacefully resist the operation of the chemical factory.

As Tirtha Roy takes back Sambaran in his custody the sun sets over Elysium, casting a golden glow across its steel and glass towers, Neem Baba and Sambaran Roy become unwavering allies. They vowed to leave no room for doubt, meticulously constructing a comprehensive report that would lay bare the crimes committed against nature. Their shared mission became a beacon of hope for the affected environment and all those yearning for justice. Once freed, Sambaran promised to do the first thing to visit the Neem Baba's ashram and have a private meeting with him as he had some doubts to clear.

With each passing day, their resolve grew stronger, and the imminent clash between power and righteousness loomed closer. The fate of Elysium hung in the balance as Neem Baba and Sambaran embarked on their quest to expose the truth, restore harmony, and rewrite the narrative of their city's destiny.

Neem Baba asked all the people to come to the Elysian campus, and he will start a hunger strike tomorrow. Until the Chemical factory doesn't stop emitting poisonous gas we decided not to stop.

"I will not let Burdwan turn it into another Bhopal"

Chapter 9: Neem Flower

14th May, 2024. Sinthala Temple

As Neem Baba's hunger strike in front of Elysian Campus started gaining momentum everything started happening wrong for Adani Corporation. First, the farmer groups of Bengal extended support to Neem Baba they came in heavy numbers from Palasrirampur and Becharhat who were the most affected by Adani's corporation's aggressive policies. Finally, the Opposition MPs and MLAs came in numbers to catch a selfie with

Neem Baba and post it on their social media profiles. Neem Baba's hunger strike becoming popular every day. In between Military was called but they failed in front of Neem Baba's resolve. The farmer group and the opposition have extended their full support to Neem Baba and the Government in backfoot.

There was the question raised in Parliament.

Finally, Neembaba broke the haradhanu to win Mother Earth in the form of "Sita". Satyananada Adani decided to shut down the Pesticide factory after his Initial Public offering was hit by a Financial report by an International Audit Company mentioning inconsistency and irregularity in financial reporting. It was hitting the news for some time and the Adani corporation had a very bad public image. Questions were again raised in Parliament.

Satyananda Adani made a YouTube video to announce the halt of the Initial Public Offering and also apologized to Neem Baba and announced compensation for the people of Burdwan who were affected by the poisonous gas emission from the Pesticide factory on the Elysian campus. He also decided to follow the NGT court order and temporarily shut down the campus which was emitting poisonous gas.

Sambaran Roy was given bail as Adani Corporation took away the defamation charges against him. He as promised came to see Neem Baba after coming out of Jail and wanted to clear some doubts which he had been holding for a long time.

"How is it possible you have no role to play in the accident of Dr Rahul Maitra even though he was coming to you ?" Sambaran Roy was surprised and he almost roared.

" Why it is not possible," Neem Baba said quietly. You don't know the facts that's why it is looking so surprising   to   you.

"It's a dam gas leak" Samabaran Roy was impatient and he continued to roar with anger. "And you are making an impossible story out of it. How can a person die in a car from that gas leak? He will drive the car and run away"

"For that, he has to understand that it's a gas leak" Neem Baba calmly added his comments with an almost fiery and angry Sambaran.

"You are hiding something. How does a normal person not understand that there was a gas leak like Mithyale Isocynate" Sambaran gave a suspicious look towards Neem Baba. But Sambaran also has not seen a person remain so cool in front of such a violent interrogation which he is doing. It seemed that Neem Baba remained unaffected by the entire emotional pressure that Sambaran had been trying to put on Neem Baba.

" What to hide. Burdwan is the rice bowl of West Bengal. There are many pesticide factories here as an agro-allied industry. It is used to manufacture pesticides. It is kept as a liquid and stored in a tank. But it is explosive and can burst. Due to climate change, the temperature this year has crossed over 45. I have often seen it has touched 47 even in our Sithala temple. With this temperature, many things can catch fire and that can make many things burst. What is so uncommon is if one of these tanks which is storing Methyale Isocynate gets bursted. You know it mixes very quickly with air and so the air can become poisonous". Neem Baba orchestrated in a slow and calm tone but his every words are very much audible.

"But the siren. What happened to Siren? If anything like that happens the factory has an automated siren system that will start creating alarms and people evacuate their houses. In my childhood, something like this happened, just 2 years after the Bhopal gas tragedy, possibly in a Satima Cold storage. There was a gas leak and there was a siren which alerted us. We used to stay in Nilpur and police came to evacuate us. There is the evacuation process and safety measures otherwise the amount of poisonous gases some of this chemical factory stores with them we will be having Bhopal tragedy now and then" Sambaran Roy confirmed that Neem Baba was hiding or missing something.

"What is so surprising if the Siren doesn't work? It's after all a mechanical device." Neem Baba was very firm in his argument.

"How are you so sure about everything" Samabaran Roy felt very uneasy with this new surprising twist on Dr Rahul Maitra's murder case. He has been wandering in his mind "Is neem baba misguiding him". He nodded inside his head on his own. The Sithala temple was becoming cooler as the shift of temperature when the hot noon was giving away to the silent and cool afternoon. Some dark clouds are also spreading across the sky.

"Because Tirtha Roy showed the postmortem report and it was death due to excessive inhalation of Mithyale Isocynate" Neem Baba kept his unusual calmness.

" But he announced in the press conference that it was Sulphur dioxide and Particular matter below 2.5 microns that was responsible for the lung failure. He never said Mithyale Isocyanate. I was there at the press conference. He was answering one of my questions. How can he lie so deliberately in the press conference?" After a long time, Sambaran felt that he had found a clue that could weaken the calm and composure of Neem Baba.

But there has been no change in Neem Baba's face. He remained as cool as he was earlier. Almost not bother with the external chaos whichever is going around you.

" He has not lied, he has been saving all of you from having a panic attack you can have with Mithyale Isocyanate revealed as the cause of death. I am sure that the heat waves due to climate change are the main cause. There are even heat waves and extreme temperatures over 46c in the night. and it can be the cause of the burst"

In the afternoon after the rain, Neem Baba was very contemplative. He observed the Neem flowers in all the branches of the Neem Tree of Sitala Mandir. The storm that was continuing to flow in his mind suddenly stopped for a moment. He uttered in his mind " Something needs to be done but what, can save these innocent lives"

Sambaran went through the entire process in his mind and found that what Neem Baba was mentioning had some valid logic and it is not just intuitive but also objective.

Epilogue

After Sambaran left Neem Baba called Soumen and asked that nobody should disturb him as plans to meditate for a long time. Soumen nodded his head and asked the attendant to take care that nobody is allowed to meet Neem Baba when he meditates.

Neem Baba sat on the lotus pose in the shade of the Neem Tree and kept his eyes closed. As soon as his eyes are closed there is heavy rain which swept the external environment of Sithala temple. Neem Baba remained absolutely oblivion about the rain. Soumen remained confused. as Neem Baba had asked him that nobody would disturb him, and so he kept standing close to Neem Baba. The rain swept him completely and his entire orange robe became wet.

As the rain grew stronger it seemed it would take away Neem Baba with a sweep. Soumen was very afraid. He started calling "Neem Baba", "Neem Baba". But Neem Baba remained in the state of Samadhi and didn't utter a single word. Soumen first to wake him up from the Samadhi tried to push him. The rain started slowing down and when the rain completely slowed down, Neem Baba opened his eyes.

Soumen almost got his life back. He shouted in joy "Neem Baba is back". The attendants and Soumen were in a state of euphoria.

But Neem Baba became quiet.

" We were so afraid that you might have died in the Samadhi."

"Don't worry my work is not done. I will not die until my work is done. As long as there is1·67 million premature deaths in India due to air pollution. This will be growing when climate change joins hands with air pollution. It will create the resulting burden of economic loss of $36·8 billion which is 1·36% of India's gross domestic product (GDP). How can my work be done ?"

" We don't want you to die. But that's a tall order to achieve."

" It's not a very tall order if we try together we can achieve it probably in the next five years" Neem Baba's face reflected a certain kind of determination which is called "Cool Virya". Virya is a property of warriors of India, who reflect determination, boldness, and success. However, with this comes also arrogance and hot-headedness. Neem Baba was always the opposite, he was silent, quiet, and cool yet very determined, very bold, and very successful."

"How?".

" If every household plans to plant one Neem Tree. There are 20 million Neem Tree in India and our population is 125 billion. The only way we can clean our air is by increasing the ratio of Neem Tree to every 1000 people. Neem is a scientifically proven plant to absorbs pollutants much more than its contemporary trees. It is a gift of the 21st century to handle two of its man-made malice – Climate Change and Air pollution. "

Authors Bio

Sri Joydip is a prolific bilingual Indian writer in English and Bengali. He writes on a vast canvas of universal, existential, and spiritual themes, with deep roots in Indian ancient culture and tradition. He also writes on contemporary themes related to social issues, managerial issues, and health and wellness issues. His writing conveys the diversity of human experience in multiple genres, including poetry, non-fiction, fiction, and travel writing.

Some of Sri Joydip's most popular works include:

"Stories from Arunachala Diaries"
"Seven Yoga Habits that can transform your life"
"Neem baba"
" Ananter Blackboard"
"Second Chance"

Sri Joydip's work has been recognized with numerous awards and appreciation, including:

1. National Novel Writing Month 2021 Winner for Diamond Fort (Historical Fiction)

2.Feminist International Journal (Petty Progressive) Hall of Fame for "Seven Yoga Habits that can transform your life"

3. Fupping Book Reviewer Zak Parker's list of 14 books on managing anxiety, which includes "Innovation@YogaEducation: Sri Joydip Ashram Story"

As a Gyan Yoga Teacher. Sri Joydip's work in the field of using Gyan Yoga for SDG3 (health and well-being of all) through the NGO founded by him– Sri Joydip Ashram Gyan Yoga Training and Research Centre has also been recognized with numerous awards, including:

1.Appreciation by the International Federation of Yoga Professionals for Sri Joydip's work on 'Yoga for ADHD' in 2017

2.Teacher Innovation Award for Sri Joydip as a Gyan Yoga Teacher by Sri Aurobindo Society and HDFC Bank for Innovative education through Joyful and Experiential learning in 2019.

3.Personal Excellence Award to Sri Joydip for his 23 years of career contribution to society, by CSR Times and India Achievers Forum in 2021.

4.A Research Paper prepared under the leadership of Sri Joydip, based on Sri Joydip's Book Neem Baba titled "Household Neem Plantation for reduction of PM2.5 and PM10" has been selected for Stage II of Life Project by Niti Aayog – Government of India in 2023.

Sri Joydip lives in Bengal, India.